The Diary of a Killer Cat

Anne Fine was born and educated in the Midlands, and now lives in County Durham. She has written numerous highly acclaimed and prize-winning books for children and adults. Her novel *The Tulip Touch* won the Whitbread Children's Book of the Year Award; *Goggle-Eyes* won the Guardian Children's Fiction Award and the Carnegie Medal, and was adapted for television by the BBC; *Flour Babies* won the Carnegie Medal and the Whitbread Children's Book Award; *Bill's New Frock* won a Smarties Prize, and *Madame Doubtfire* has become a major feature film.

Anne Fine was named Children's Laureate in 2001.

www.annefine.co.uk

D1354008

Anne Fine
The Diary of a
Killer Cat

Illustrated by Steve Cox

PUFFIN

PUFFIN BOOKS

Published by the Penguin Group
Penguin Books Ltd, 80 Strand, London WC2R 0RL, England
Penguin Group (USA) Inc., 375 Hudson Street, New York, New York 10014, USA
Penguin Group Australia, 250 Camberwell Road, Camberwell,
Victoria 3124, Australia
Penguin Books Canada Ltd, 10 Alcorn Avenue, Toronto, Ontario, Canada M4V 3B2
Penguin Books Inida (P) Ltd, 11 Community Centre, Panchsheel Park,
New Delhi – 110 017, India
Penguin Group (NZ), cnr Airborne and Rosedale Roads, Albany,
Auckland 1310, New Zealand
Penguin Books (South Africa) (Pty) Ltd, 24 Sturdee Avenue, Rosebank, 2196,
South Africa

Penguin Books Ltd, Registered Offices: 80 Strand, London WC2R 0RL, England

www.penguin.com

First published by Hamish Hamilton Ltd 1994
Published in Puffin Books 1996
Published in this edition 2004
This edition published 2010 for The Book People Ltd,
Hall Wood Avenue, Haydock, St Helens, WA11 9UL
1

Text copyright © Anne Fine, 1994
Illustrations copyright © Steve Cox, 1994
Introduction copyright © Julia Eccleshare, 2004
All rights reserved

The moral right of the authors and illustrator has been asserted

Set in 17/20 Bembo
Made and printed in England by Clays Ltd, St Ives plc

British Library Cataloguing in Publication Data
A CIP catalogue record for this book is available from the British Library

ISBN: 978-0-141-33703-6

www.greenpenguin.co.uk

Penguin Books is committed to a sustainable future
for our business, our readers and our planet.
The book in your hands is made from paper
certified by the Forest Stewardship Council.

INTRODUCTION

BY JULIA ECCLESHARE, SERIES EDITOR

Can you imagine being right inside your cat's head? That is exactly where you are in *The Diary of a Killer Cat*. Once you've read this book, you'll be able to see everything from a new point of view. Think how horrible it is to be stuck in a cage waiting for the vet – especially with a tasty-looking gerbil sitting nearby. Or to be labelled HANDLE WITH CARE. Or to be accused of a crime you haven't even committed. Poor pussycat! But don't let the Killer Cat deceive you. Okay, so a cat can be soft and cuddly and furry, but inside every soft pussycat, there's a cunning little beast.

After I'd read *The Diary of a Killer Cat*, I never saw a cat in quite the same way again. I now realize that a cat knows what you are thinking – even if you haven't said it. It knows what you hate and what you like about it – and, mostly, it just doesn't care! Above all, don't ever think that you are in charge of a cat. For every plan you have, a cat will have one to outsmart you . . .

Anne Fine stands up for cats in this hilarious story of humans, cats, gerbils, dogs – and a somewhat unfortunate rabbit . . .

Okay, okay. So hang me. I killed the bird. For pity's sake, I'm a *cat*. It's practically my *job* to go creeping round the garden after sweet little eensy-weensy birdy-pies that can hardly fly from one hedge to another. So what am I supposed to do when one of the poor feathery little flutterballs just about throws itself into my mouth? I mean, it practically landed on my paws. It could have *hurt* me.

Okay, *okay*. So I biffed it. Is that any reason for Ellie to cry in my fur so hard I almost *drown,* and squeeze me so hard I almost *choke*?

'Oh, Tuffy!' she says, all sniffles and red eyes and piles of wet tissues. 'Oh, Tuffy. How could you *do* that?'

How could I *do* that? I'm a *cat*. How did I know there was going to be such a giant great fuss, with Ellie's mother rushing off to fetch sheets of old

newspaper, and Ellie's father filling a bucket with soapy water?

Okay, *okay.* So maybe I shouldn't have dragged it in and left it on the carpet. And maybe the stains won't come out, ever.

So *hang* me.

2: TUESDAY

I quite enjoyed the little funeral. I don't think they really wanted me to come, but, after all, it's just as much my garden as theirs. In fact, I spend a whole lot more time in it than they do. I'm the only one in the family who uses it properly.

Not that they're grateful. You ought to hear them.

'That cat is *ruining* my flower beds. There are hardly any of the petunias left.'

'I'd barely *planted* the lobelias before it was lying on top of them, squashing them flat.'

'I *do* wish it wouldn't dig holes in the anemones.'

Moan, moan, moan, moan. I don't know why they bother to keep a cat, since all they ever seem to do is complain.

All except Ellie. She was too busy being soppy about the bird. She put it in a box, and packed it round with cotton wool, and dug a little hole, and then we all stood round it while she said a few words, wishing the bird luck in heaven.

'Go away,' Ellie's father hissed at me. (I find that man quite rude.) But I just flicked my tail at him. Gave him the blink. Who does he think he is? If I want to watch a little birdy's funeral, I'll watch it. After all, I've known the bird longer than any of them have. I knew it when it was *alive*.

3 : WEDNESDAY

So spank me! I brought a dead mouse into their precious house. I didn't even kill it. When I came across it, it was already a goner. Nobody's safe around here. This avenue is ankle-deep in rat poison, fast cars charge up and down at all hours, and I'm not the only cat around here. I don't even know what happened to the thing. All I know is, I found it. It was already dead. (Fresh dead, but dead.) And at the time I thought it was a good idea to bring it home. Don't ask me why. I must have been crazy. How did I know that Ellie was going to grab me and give me one of her little talks?

'Oh, Tuffy! That's the second time this week. I can't bear it. I know you're a cat, and it's natural and everything. But please, for my sake, stop.'

She gazed into my eyes.

'Will you stop? Please?'

I gave her the blink. (Well, I tried. But she wasn't having any.)

'I *mean* it, Tuffy,' she told me. 'I love you, and I understand how you feel. But you've got to stop doing this, okay?'

She had me by the paws. What could I say? So I tried to look all sorry. And then she burst into tears all over again, and we had another funeral.

This place is turning into Fun City. It really is.

Okay, okay! I'll try and explain about the rabbit. For starters, I don't think anyone's given me enough credit for getting it through the cat flap. That was *not easy*. I can tell you, it took about an hour to get that rabbit through that little hole. That rabbit was downright *fat*. It was more like a pig than a rabbit, if you want my opinion.

Not that any of them cared what I thought. They were going mental.

'It's Thumper!' cried Ellie. 'It's next-door's Thumper!'

'Oh, Lordy!' said Ellie's father. 'Now

we're in trouble. What are we going to do?'

Ellie's mother stared at me.

'How could a cat *do* that?' she asked. 'I mean, it's not like a tiny bird, or a mouse, or anything. That rabbit is the same size as Tuffy. They both weigh a *ton*.'

Nice. Very nice. This is my *family*, I'll have you know. Well, Ellie's family. But you take my point.

And Ellie, of course, freaked out. She went berserk.

'It's horrible,' she cried. '*Horrible*. I can't believe that Tuffy could have done that. Thumper's been next door for years and years and years.'

Sure. Thumper was a friend. I knew him well.

She turned on me.

'Tuffy! This is the end. That poor, poor rabbit. Look at him!'

And Thumper did look a bit of a mess, I admit it. I mean, most of it was only mud. And a few grass stains, I suppose. And there were quite a few bits of twig and stuff stuck in his fur. And he had a streak of oil on one ear. But no one gets dragged the whole way across a garden, and through a hedge, and over another garden, and through a freshly-oiled cat flap, and ends up looking as if they're just off to a party.

And Thumper didn't care what he looked like. He was *dead*.

The rest of them minded, though. They minded a *lot*.

'What are we going to do?'

'Oh, this is dreadful. Next-door will never speak to us again.'

'We must think of something.'

And they did. I have to say, it was a

brilliant plan, by any standards. First, Ellie's father fetched the bucket again, and filled it with warm soapy water. (He gave me a bit of a look as he did this, trying to make me feel guilty for the fact that he'd had to dip his hands in the old Fairy Liquid twice in one week. I just gave him my old 'I-am-not-impressed' stare back.)

Then Ellie's mother dunked Thumper in the bucket and gave him a nice bubbly wash and a swill-about. The water turned a pretty nasty brown colour. (All that mud.) And then, glaring at me as if it were all *my* fault, they tipped it down the sink and began over again with fresh soap suds.

Ellie was snivelling, of course.

'Do stop that, Ellie,' her mother said. 'It's getting on my nerves. If you want to

do something useful, go and fetch the hairdrier.'

So Ellie trailed upstairs, still bawling her eyes out.

I sat on the top of the dresser, and watched them.

They up-ended poor Thumper and dunked him again in the bucket. (Good job he wasn't his old self. He'd have hated all this washing.) And when the water finally ran clear, they pulled him out and drained him.

Then they plonked him on newspaper, and gave Ellie the hairdrier.

'There you go,' they said. 'Fluff him up nicely.'

Well, she got right into it, I can tell you. That Ellie could grow up to be a real hot-shot hairdresser, the way she fluffed him up. I have to say, I never saw Thumper look so nice before, and he lived in next-door's hutch for years and years, and I saw him every day.

'Hiya, Thump,' I'd sort of nod at him as I strolled over the lawn to check out what was left in the feeding bowls further down the avenue.

'Hi, Tuff,' he'd sort of twitch back.

Yes, we were good mates. We were pals. And so it was really nice to see him looking so spruced up and smart when Ellie had finished with him.

He looked *good*.

'What now?' said Ellie's father.

Ellie's mum gave him a look – the sort of look she sometimes gives me, only nicer.

'Oh, no,' he said. 'Not me. Oh, no, no, no, no, no.'

'It's you or me,' she said. 'And I can't go, can I?'

'Why not?' he said. 'You're smaller than I am. You can crawl through the hedge easier.'

That's when I realized what they had in mind. But what could I say? What could I do to stop them? To *explain*?

Nothing. I'm just a cat.

I sat and watched.

5: FRIDAY

I call it Friday because they left it so late. The clock was already well past midnight by the time Ellie's father finally heaved himself out of his comfy chair in front of the telly and went upstairs. When he came down again he was dressed in black. Black from head to foot.

'You look like a cat burglar,' said Ellie's mother.

'I wish someone would burgle *our* cat,' he muttered.

I just ignored him. I thought that was best.

Together they went to the back door.

'Don't switch the outside light on,' he warned her. 'You never know who might be watching.'

I tried to sneak out at the same time, but Ellie's mother held me back with her foot.

'You can just stay inside tonight,' she told me. 'We've had enough trouble from you this week.'

Fair's fair. And I heard all about it anyway, later, from Bella and Tiger and Pusskins. They all reported back. (They're good mates.) They all saw Ellie's father creeping across the lawn, with his plastic bag full of Thumper (wrapped nicely in a towel to keep him clean). They all saw him forcing his way through the hole in the hedge, and crawling across next-door's lawn on his tummy.

'Couldn't think *what* he was doing,' Pusskins said afterwards.

'*Ruined* the hole in the hedge,' complained Bella. 'He's made it so big that the Thompson's rottweiler could get through it now.'

'That father of Ellie's must have the most dreadful night vision,' said Tiger. 'It took him forever to find that hutch in the dark.'

'And prise the door open.'

'And stuff in poor old Thumper.'

'And set him out neatly on his bed of straw.'

'All curled up.'

'With the straw patted up round him.'

'So it looked as if he was sleeping.'

'It was very, very lifelike,' said Bella. 'It could have fooled me. If anyone just happened to be passing in the dark, they'd really have thought that poor old Thumper had just died happily and peacefully in his sleep, after a good life, from old age.'

They all began howling with laughter.

'Sshh!' I said. 'Keep it down, guys. They'll hear, and I'm not supposed to be out tonight. I'm grounded.'

They all stared at me.

'Get away with you!'

'Grounded?'

'What *for*?'

'Murder,' I said. 'For cold-blooded bunnicide.'

That set us all off again. We yowled and yowled. The last I heard before we took off in a gang up Beechcroft Drive was one of the bedroom windows being flung open, and Ellie's father yelling, 'How did you get out, you crafty beast?'

So what's he going to do? Nail up the cat flap?

He nailed up the cat flap. Would you *believe* this man? He comes down the stairs this morning, and before he's even out of his pyjamas he's set to work with the hammer and a nail.

Bang, bang, bang, bang!

I'm giving him the stare, I really am. But then he turns round and speaks to me directly.

'There,' he says. 'That'll fix you. Now it swings *this* way −' He gives the cat flap a hefty shove with his foot. 'But it doesn't swing *this* way.'

And, sure enough, when the flap

tried to flap back in, it couldn't. It hit the nail.

'So,' he says to me. 'You can go out. Feel free to go out. Feel free, in fact, not only to go out, but also to stay out, get lost, or disappear for ever. But should you bother to come back again, don't go to the trouble of bringing anything with you. Because this is now a one-way flap, and so you will have to sit on the doormat until one of the family lets you in.'

He narrows his eyes at me, all nasty-like.

'And woe betide you, Tuffy, if there's anything dead lying waiting on the doormat beside you.'

'Woe betide you'! What a stupid expression. What on earth does it mean anyway? 'Woe betide you'!

Woe betide *him*.

I hate Saturday morning. It's so unsettling, all that fussing and door-banging and 'Have you got the purse?' and 'Where's the shopping list?' and 'Do we need catfood?' Of course we need catfood. What else am I supposed to eat all week? Air?

They were all pretty quiet today,

though. Ellie was sitting at the table carving Thumper a rather nice gravestone out of half a leftover cork floor tile. It said:

Thumper
Rest in peace

'You mustn't take it round next-door yet,' her father warned her. 'Not till they've told us Thumper's dead, at any rate.'

Some people are born soft. Her eyes brimmed with tears.

'There goes Next-door now,' Ellie's mother said, looking out of the window.

'Which way is she headed?'

'Towards the shops.'

'Good. If we keep well behind, we can get Tuffy to the vet's without bumping into her.'

Tuffy? Vet's?

Ellie was even more horrified than I was. She threw herself at her father, beating him with her soft little fists.

'Dad! No! You can't!'

I put up a far better fight with my claws. When he finally prised me out of the dark of the cupboard under the sink, his woolly was ruined and his hands were scratched and bleeding all over.

He wasn't very pleased about it.

'Come out of there, you great fat

furry psychopath. It's only a 'flu jab you're booked in for – more's the pity!'

Would *you* have believed him? I wasn't absolutely sure. (Neither was Ellie, so she tagged along.) I was still quite suspicious when we reached the vet's. That is *the only reason* why I spat at the girl behind the desk. There was no reason on earth to write HANDLE WITH CARE at the top of my case notes. Even the Thompson's rottweiler doesn't have HANDLE WITH CARE written on the top of his case notes. What's wrong with *me*?

So I was a little rude in the waiting room. So what? I *hate* waiting. And I especially hate waiting stuffed in a wire cat cage. It's cramped. It's hot. And it's boring. After a few hundred minutes of sitting there quietly, *anyone* would start teasing their neighbours. I didn't *mean* to frighten that little sick baby gerbil half to death. I was only *looking* at it. It's a free country, isn't it? Can't a cat even *look* at a sweet little baby gerbil?

And if I was licking my lips (which I wasn't) that's only because I was thirsty. Honestly. I wasn't trying to pretend I was going to eat it.

The trouble with baby gerbils is they can't take a *joke*.

And neither can anyone else round here.

Ellie's father looked up from the pamphlet he was reading called *'Your Pet and Worms'*. (Oh, nice. Very nice.)

'Turn the cage round the other way, Ellie,' he said.

Ellie turned my cage round the other way.

Now I was looking at the Fisher's terrier. (And if there's any animal in the world who ought to have HANDLE WITH CARE written at the top of his case notes, it's the Fisher's terrier.)

Okay, so I hissed at him. It was only a little hiss. You practically had to have bionic ears to *hear* it.

And I did growl a bit. But you'd think he'd have a head start on growling. He is a dog, after all. I'm only a cat.

And yes, okay, I spat a bit. But only a

bit. Nothing you'd even *notice* unless you were waiting to pick on someone.

Well, how was *I* to know he wasn't feeling very well? Not *everyone* waiting for the vet is ill. *I* wasn't ill, was I? Actually, I've never been ill in my life. I don't even know what it *feels* like. But I reckon, even if I were *dying,* something furry locked in a cage could make an eensy-weensy noise at me without my

ending up whimpering and cowering, and scrabbling to get under the seat, to hide behind the knees of my owner.

More a *chicken* than a Scotch terrier, if you want my opinion.

'Could you please keep that vile cat of yours under control?' Mrs Fisher said nastily.

Ellie stuck up for me.

'He is in a cage!'

'He's still scaring half the animals in here to death. Can't you cover him up, or something?'

Ellie was going to keep arguing, I could tell. But, without even looking up from his worm pamphlet, her father just dropped his raincoat over my cage as if I were some mangy old *parrot* or something.

And everything went black.

No wonder by the time the vet came at me with her nasty long needle, I was in a bit of a mood. I didn't mean to scratch her that badly, though.

Or smash all those little glass bottles.

Or tip the expensive new cat scales off the bench.

Or spill all that cleaning fluid.

It wasn't me who ripped my record card into tiny pieces, though. That was the vet.

When we left, Ellie was in tears again. She hugged my cage tightly to her chest.

'Oh, Tuffy! Until we find a new vet who'll promise to look after you, you must be so careful not to get run over.'

'Fat chance!' her father muttered.

I was just glowering at him through the cage wire, when he spotted Ellie's mother, standing knee-deep in shopping bags outside the supermarket.

'You're very late,' she scolded. 'Was there a bit of trouble at the vet's?'

Ellie burst into tears. I mean, talk about *wimp*. But her father is made of sterner stuff. He'd just taken the most huge breath, ready to snitch on me, when suddenly he let it out again. Out of the corner of his eye, he'd spotted trouble of another sort.

'Quick!' he whispered. 'Next-door is just coming through the check-out.'

He picked up half the shopping bags. Ellie's mother picked up the rest. But before we could get away, Next-door had come through the glass doors.

So now all four of them were forced to chat.

'Morning,' said Ellie's father.

'Morning,' said Next-door.

'Nice day,' said Ellie's father.

'Lovely,' agreed Next-door.

'Nicer than yesterday,' said Ellie's mother.

'Oh, yes,' Next-door said. 'Yesterday was *horrible*.'

She probably just meant the weather, for heaven's sake. But Ellie's eyes filled with tears. (I don't know why she was so fond of Thumper. *I'm* the one who's supposed to be her pet, not *him.)* And because she couldn't see where she was going properly any more, she bumped into her mother, and half the tins of catfood fell out of one of the shopping bags, and rolled off down the street.

Ellie dumped down my cage, and chased off after them. Then she made the mistake of reading the labels.

'Oh, nooo!' she wailed. 'Rabbit chunks!'

(Really, that child is such a *drip*. She'd never make it in our gang. She wouldn't last a *week*.)

'Talking about rabbit,' said Next-door. 'The most extraordinary thing happened at our house.'

'Really?' said Ellie's father, glaring at me.

'Oh, yes?' said Ellie's mother, glaring at me as well.

'Yes,' said Next-door. 'On Monday, poor Thumper looked a little bit poorly, so we brought him inside. And on

Tuesday, he was worse. And on Wednesday he died. He was terribly old, and he'd had a happy life, so we didn't feel too bad about it. In fact we had a little funeral, and buried him in a box at the bottom of the garden.'

I'm staring up at the clouds now.

'And on Thursday, he'd gone.'

'Gone?'

'Gone?'

'Yes, gone. And all there was left of him was a hole in the ground and an empty box.'

'Really?'

'Good heavens!'

Ellie's father was giving me the most suspicious look.

'And then, yesterday,' Next-door went on. 'Something even more extraordinary happened. Thumper was back again. All fluffed up nicely, and back in his hutch.'

'Back in his hutch, you say?'

'Fluffed up nicely? How strange!'

You have to hand it to them, they're good actors. They kept it up all the way home.

'What an amazing story!'

'How on earth could it have happened?'

'Quite astonishing!'

'So strange!'

Till we were safely through the front door. And then, of course, the pair of them turned on me.

'Deceitful creature!'

'Making us think you killed him!'

'Just pretending all along!'

'I *knew* that cat could never have done it. That rabbit was even fatter than he is!'

You'd have thought they all *wanted* me to have murdered old Thumper.

All except Ellie. She was *sweet*.

'Don't you *dare* pick on Tuffy!' she told them. 'You leave him alone! I bet he didn't even dig poor Thumper up. I bet it was the Fisher's nasty, vicious terrier who did that. All Tuffy did was bring Thumper back to us so we could make sure he was buried again properly. He's a hero. A kind and thoughtful hero.'

She gave me a big soft squeeze.

'Isn't that right, Tuffy?'

I'm saying nothing, am I? I'm a cat. So I just sat and watched while they unnailed the cat flap.